# THE
# TIME
# MACHINE

# THE
# TIME
# MACHINE

by
## *H. G. Wells*

Adapted by
C. Louise March

Illustrated by
Julia Lundman

Modern Publishing
A Division of Unisystems, Inc.
New York, New York 10022

Series UPC: 38150

Cover art by Bob Berry

# Contents

$\P$

# CHAPTER 1
# THE TIME TRAVELER

The Time Traveler, as I've come to remember him, was eagerly explaining to us his new insight into the nature of time. His gray eyes shone, and his usually pale face was flushed and very animated. But the fire burned brightly in the fireplace, and the cozy chairs, which our host had invented, caused our minds to wander. We were used to his fondness for scientific mysteries and debate. But he pointed his finger at us and offered us a new curiosity.

"You must follow me carefully," he

said. "I will have to challenge some ideas that are almost universally accepted. The geometry that you learned in school is incorrect."

The six guests looked at the Time Traveler. The Doctor, the Psychologist, the Mayor, a quiet young man and I all remained silent. But Filby, who liked to argue, said, "That's quite an extravagant statement to make!"

"There are grounds for this theory. Some things can be measured in three

dimensions: length, width, and height," the Time Traveler said. "But there is a fourth dimension. Without this fourth dimension, everything is but an idea in the mind of man."

Filby began to argue again, until the Time Traveler explained that the fourth dimension is time.

"Clearly, any real body must have length, breadth, thickness and duration. The problem is that time has no physical existence. The other dimensions can be measured in space," he explained. "We remember the past and we can imagine the future. Even though the events in our minds do not occupy space in the usual way, they do exist—in time. Have all of you heard what the experts have to say about this fourth dimension?"

The Mayor admitted that he had not.

"Space is described as having three dimensions. But some researchers have tried to construct a four-dimensional geometry. We know that on a flat surface, which has only two dimensions, we can represent a figure of a three-dimensional solid. Similarly some think that with three-dimensional models we can represent something that, in reality, consists of four." He paused.

The Doctor stared hard into the fire. He said, "If time is really only a fourth dimension of space, why can't we move in time as we move about in the other three dimensions? Men cannot move at all in time. They cannot get away from the present moment."

The Time Traveler's face lit up. "You're wrong. We are always running away from the present movement. Our mental existences, which have no physical substance, move freely in time."

"You can move about in all directions of space. But you cannot move about in time," the Psychologist interrupted.

"That is the essence of my great discovery," said the Time Traveler. "If man can defy gravity in a balloon, why should he not hope to be able to stop or accelerate his movement in time?" the Time Traveler asked.

"This is ridiculous," said Filby. "You will never convince me until I see it."

"Long ago I had a vision of a machine," the Time Traveler said. "That machine could travel in any direction of space and time, as the driver determined."

Filby laughed.

"Don't laugh yet," the Time Traveler cut in. "I have been working on an

experiment to verify the possibility of traveling through time."

"It would be a great help to historians," the Psychologist suggested. "One could travel back to the Middle Ages or see dinosaurs in prehistoric times!"

"Then there is the future," said the Young Man. "One could travel forward to see whom one will marry or what stock to buy."

The Time Traveler smiled at us. He walked slowly out of the room, and we heard his slippers shuffling down the hallway leading to his laboratory.

"I wonder what he's up to," said the Psychologist.

"Some trick or other, no doubt," said the Doctor.

The Time Traveler was generally known to be a man of superior intellect and daring. But most of his friends also knew of his love of drama. It is no surprise that we were all skeptical about his experiment.

When he returned, the Time Traveler held a glittering metallic mechanism. It was scarcely larger than a small clock, and very delicately made. There was ivory in it, and some transparent, crystal-like substance. He placed the mechanism on a small table, around which we gathered for a closer look. The only other object on the table was a small lamp. There were also a number of candles lit, so that the room was brilliantly illuminated.

"This little model," said the Time

Traveler, resting his elbows upon the table and pressing his hands together above the thing, "will give you an idea of my plan for a machine to travel through time. You will notice that it looks off balance. There is an odd twinkling appearance about this bar. And these little white levers are quite important."

The Doctor got out of his chair and examined it closely. "It's beautifully made," he said.

"It took two years to make," said the Time Traveler. "Pressing this lever sends the machine gliding into the future. The other lever reverses the motion. This saddle is the seat. I am now going to press the lever, and off the machine will go. It will vanish, pass into the future, and disappear. Have a good look at the thing. Look at the table, too, and satisfy yourselves that there is no trickery."

Then the Time Traveler moved one finger toward the lever. "No," he said

suddenly. "Give me your hand." And turning to the Psychologist, the Time Traveler told him to put out his forefinger. Thus, it was the Psychologist who sent forth the model Time Machine on its way into the future. There was a breath of wind. The lamp flame flickered. One of the candles on the mantel was blown out. The little machine swung round, became a shadow, and then was gone! Except for the lamp, the table was bare.

Everyone was silent for a minute.

Then Filby said he was stumped. The Psychologist recovered from his shock and looked under the table. The Time Traveler laughed cheerfully.

We stared at one another. "Are you serious about this?" the Doctor asked. "Do you really believe that your machine has traveled into time?"

"Certainly," said the Time Traveler confidently. "What is more, I have a full-scale machine nearly finished in my laboratory. And soon it will be ready to take

me on a journey through time."

"Are you saying that the model has traveled into the future?" asked Filby.

"I don't know for certain if it has gone into the future or the past," the Time Traveler said. "Would you like to see the Time Machine itself?" With that, he took up the lamp and led the way down the long, drafty corridor to his laboratory. We followed him with puzzled looks on our faces. In the laboratory, we saw a larger version of the little mechanism

that had vanished before our eyes. Parts were made of nickel, parts of ivory, and parts had been filed or cut out of rock crystal. It seemed nearly finished, but the levers—twisted crystalline bars— were laid on a bench beside some sheets of drawings. I took one up for a better look at it.

"Are you perfectly serious?" asked the Doctor. "Or is this a trick like that ghost you showed us last Christmas?"

"Upon that machine," said the Time Traveler determinedly, holding the lamp over it, "I intend to travel through time."

I caught Filby's eye over the shoulder of the Doctor. He winked at me.

I don't think any of us said very much about time traveling from that evening until the following week. Seven days after the Time Traveler described his remarkable ideas, and revealed to us his incredible machine, we came together once again at the Time Traveler's home. But, though we said nothing to

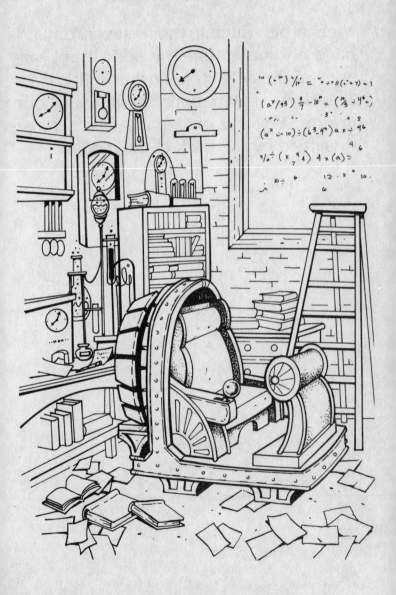

each other during those seven days, I have no doubt that the odd disappearance of the delicate model and the Time Traveler's explanations remained in our minds. For my own part, I was most unsettled by the trick of the model.

# CHAPTER 2
# UNAVOIDABLY DETAINED

The next Thursday, I went again to the Time Traveler's house. I arrived late and found four or five men already gathered in the drawing room. The Doctor was standing in front of the fire with a sheet of paper in one hand and his watch in the other.

Not seeing the Time Traveler, I asked his whereabouts.

"It's rather odd," the Doctor replied. "This note here says he's unavoidably detained. He asks us to dine at seven if he's not back. He'll explain when he comes."

The Psychologist was the only person besides the Doctor and I who had attended the previous dinner. The Editor of a well-known daily paper and a Journalist were also there.

There was some speculation at the dinner table about the Time Traveler's absence. I suggested, half-jokingly, that he was traveling through time. The Editor wanted an explanation. The Psychologist volunteered an account of the "ingenious trick" we had witnessed the previous week.

In the middle of the story, the door from the hallway opened noiselessly. Our host had arrived! As the door opened wider, the Time Traveler stood before us. His shaky appearance made me cry out.

"Good heavens! What's the matter?" the Doctor shouted. Then the whole party turned toward the door.

The Time Traveler's coat was dusty and dirty and smeared with green all

down the sleeves. His hair stuck out a bit wildly, and it seemed to be grayer. His face was ghastly pale. His chin had a half-healed cut on it. He hesitated in the doorway before coming into the room. I noticed that he walked with a limp.

"What on earth have you been up to?" asked the Doctor.

The Time Traveler seemed not to understand. "Don't let me disturb you," he said. "I'm all right." He held out his glass for some water and gulped it down. His eyes grew brighter. Some color came back into his cheeks. His glance flickered over our faces and then moved around the room. "I'm going to wash and dress. Then I'll come down and explain things," he said slowly.

The Editor started to ask a question. "I'll tell you the whole story before long," the Time Traveler said firmly.

He put down his glass and walked up the staircase. Standing, I saw his feet as he went out. They were bare but for a pair of tattered and blood-stained socks. I had half a mind to follow, but I remembered how he hated any fuss about himself. I brought my attention back to the dinner table.

The Doctor was the first to recover from the shock of seeing our friend so distressed. The company began to speculate on the state of our host. "I feel assured it's this business of the

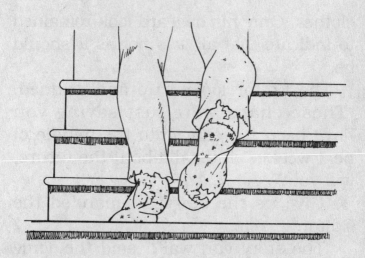

Time Machine," I said.

The Editor raised objections. "A man couldn't cover himself with dust by rolling in a mystery, could he?" And then, as the meaning came home to him, he began to joke. "Don't they have any clothes-brushes in the future?" he asked. The Journalist also would not believe it at any price. He joined the Editor in ridiculing the notion.

Just then, the Time Traveler returned, dressed in ordinary evening clothes. Only his haggard look remained to indicate that all was not as it should be.

The Editor looked up and grinned. "These chaps were just saying you have been traveling into the middle of next week! Tell us all about the future, will you?"

"Give us the story!" demanded the Editor.

"The story can wait!" said the Time Traveler. "I want something to eat. I won't say a word until I get some prop-

er nourishment."

"One word," I said impatiently. "Have you been time traveling?"

"Yes," said the Time Traveler, with his mouth full, nodding his head.

The rest of the dinner was uncomfortable. The Time Traveler devoted his attention to his dinner. It seemed as if he hadn't eaten for a week. At last he pushed his plate away and looked around the table. "I've had a most amazing time," he announced. "Let us go into the other room. It's too long a

story to tell over dirty plates." And ringing the bell for the servants, he led the way into the adjoining room.

"Have you told our new guests about the machine?" he asked me, leaning back in his chair.

"The idea is absurd!" the Editor proclaimed.

"I don't mind telling you the story, but I can't argue," the Time Traveler said. "You most likely won't believe it. So be it! It's true—every word. I was in my laboratory at four o'clock this afternoon. Since then I've lived eight days . . . such days as no human being has ever lived before! I'm nearly worn out, but I won't sleep until I've told you. But no interruptions! Is it agreed?"

"Agreed," said the Editor, and the rest of us nodded. And with that, the Time Traveler began his story as I relate it here. As he spoke, his weariness seemed to disappear. He became animated by the memory of his adventures.

Most of us were in shadow, for the candles in the drawing room had not been lit. At first we glanced now and again at one another. After a time, the Time Traveler's face and voice kept us riveted by his fascinating tale. Although it will likely sound too fantastic to believe, the intensity of our friend's expression and the sincerity in his voice held the ring of truth. This is his story.

# CHAPTER 3

# INTO THE FUTURE

Some of you have heard about the principles of the Time Machine and have seen the thing itself, incomplete in the workshop. There it is now, a little travel-worn. One of the ivory bars is cracked, and a brass rail is bent. But the rest of it is sound enough.

I expected to finish it on Friday. But just when I thought it was done, I found that one of the nickel bars was exactly one inch too short. I made the adjustment, and the machine was completed this morning. I gave it a last tap, tried all the screws again, put one more drop of oil on the quartz rod, and sat in the saddle. I took the starting lever in one hand and the stopping one in the other, pressed the first and, almost immediately, the second. I felt a terrifying sensation of falling. Looking around, I saw the laboratory exactly as before. Had anything happened? For a moment I suspected that my mind had tricked me. Then I looked at the clock. A moment before, it had stood at a minute or so past ten. Now it was nearly half-past

three!

I drew a breath, set my teeth, gripped the starting lever with both hands, and went off with a thud. The laboratory grew hazy and went dark. My housekeeper came in. She walked toward the garden door. She seemed not to see me. I suppose it took her a minute or so to walk there. But to me she seemed to shoot across the room like a rocket.

I pressed the lever over to its extreme position. The night came like the blowing out of a lamp, and in another moment the sun arose again. The laboratory had disappeared and tomorrow night came. Then day came again, then night again, then day. My mind clouded over, becoming fuzzy and confused.

I am afraid I cannot convey the peculiar sensations of time traveling. It feels as though one is falling uncontrollably forward, with a horrible anticipation of a crash. As my speed increased, night followed day like the flapping of a black wing. I saw the sun hopping swiftly across the sky, leaping it every minute, and every minute marking a day. I supposed the laboratory had been destroyed and I had been catapulted into the sky. The slowest snail that ever crawled dashed by too fast for me. The twinkling succession of darkness and light was very painful to my eyes.

Then, in the intermittent darkness, I saw the moon spinning swiftly through its phases, from quarter to new to full. As I went on, still gaining velocity, the alternation of night and day merged into one continuous gray. The sky turned a wonderful deep shade of blue, like early twilight. The sun became a streak of fire, a brilliant arc, in space.

I was still on the hillside, upon which this house now stands. I saw trees growing and changing like puffs of vapor. They grew, spread, and passed away. The whole surface of the earth seemed changed—melting and flowing

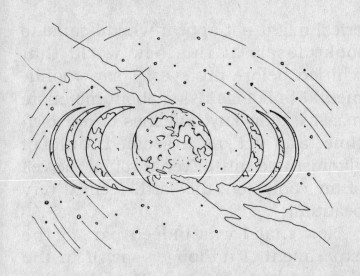

before my eyes. The little hands upon the dials that registered my speed raced around faster and faster. I noted that the sun belt swayed up and down, from season to season, in a minute or less. My pace was more than a year a minute.

At first I didn't think of stopping. I couldn't think of anything but these new sensations. But at last, my mind was overtaken by curiosity and a certain dread. What strange developments of humanity, what great discoveries, might not appear when I came to look closely at this new world that whirled before my eyes! I saw monumental buildings rising about me, more massive than any buildings of our own time, and yet, as it seemed, built of glimmer and mist. Even through the veil of my confusion, the earth seemed very beautiful.

Now that I was indeed part of the experiment, I no longer saw it in the same spirit of adventure. The fact is that the strangeness of everything, the jarring and swaying of the machine, and the feeling of prolonged falling had unnerved me. I told myself that I could never stop. Refusing to accept this, I resolved to stop immediately. Impatiently I pulled on the lever, and the machine turned over, flinging me headlong through the air.

I heard the clap of thunder, and then a shower of hail fell around me. I sat on soft grass beside the machine, which

was now turned upside down. I lay on what seemed to be a lawn in a garden, surrounded by rhododendron bushes. The hail ricocheted about me. In a moment I was soaked.

I stood up and looked around me for shelter. An enormous figure, carved from what seemed to be white stone, loomed beyond the bushes through the hazy downpour. The rest of the landscape was a blur.

As the onslaught of hail grew thinner, I saw the white figure more clearly. It was very large, for a silver birch tree

touched its shoulder. It was shaped like a winged White Sphinx. But the wings, instead of extending vertically from the sides, were spread so that the figure seemed to hover. It stood on a pedestal, which was made of bronze and was crusted over with a thick coating of green pigment.

The figure faced me, and its vacant eyes seemed to watch me. There was the faint shadow of a smile on the lips. It was greatly weather worn and falling into ruin. At last I tore my eyes from it for a moment and saw that the sky held the promise of sun.

The sheer boldness of my terrific voyage overwhelmed me. What did this strange new world hold? What had happened to men? What if cruelty had replaced reason? I might appear as a savage to the people who lived here. Was my life in danger?

In the brightening light, I saw other vast shapes—huge buildings with intricate walls and tall columns. A wooded hillside lay in the background. Fear gripped my heart. I turned frantically to the Time Machine to set it upright and see if it was in working order. The huge buildings around me stood out clear and distinct, glistening as the water left by the storm evaporated in the sun.

I felt naked in a strange world. My fear grew to frenzy. I took a deep breath and tried to start the machine. It turned over and struck my chin violently. One hand on the saddle, the other on the

lever, I stood panting heavily, ready to try again. The possibility of escape bolstered my courage. I paused to look more curiously and less fearfully at this world of the remote future. The gauge on my machine told me I was in the year Eight Hundred and Two Thousand, Seven Hundred and One!

In a circular opening, high up in the wall of the nearest house, I saw a group of figures dressed in elegant soft robes looking down at me. Then I heard voices approaching. Some of the creatures were running through the bushes near the

White Sphinx. One led the way toward my machine and me. He—or so it seemed to be a man—was a slight creature, four feet high, dressed in a purple tunic, wrapped at the waist with a leather belt. He wore sandals on his feet. His legs were bare to the knees, and his head had no covering, for it was unusually warm. He was a very beautiful and graceful creature, but looked vulnerable and frail. At the sight of him I suddenly regained confidence.

# CHAPTER 4

# THE FUTURE OF MANKIND

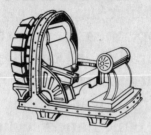

Soon we were standing face-to-face. He came straight up to me, laughed softly, and looked into my eyes. He was unafraid. Then he turned to the two others who were following him. He spoke to them in a strange and very pleasant language.

We were joined by a little group of these fine creatures. One of them spoke directly to me. It occurred to me that my voice would be too harsh and deep for them. So I shook my head and, pointing to my ears, shook it again. He came a step forward, hesitated, and

**47**

then touched my hand. Then I felt other soft little fingers upon my back and shoulders. They wanted to make sure I was real. Their graceful gentleness and childlike openness reassured me. They looked so frail that I could easily defend myself if necessary. But I made a sudden motion to warn them when I saw their little pink hands feeling the Time Machine. I unscrewed the little levers that would set it in motion. I put these in my pocket, thus protecting my means of departure. Then I turned again to resume our attempts to communicate.

These creatures had some odd characteristics. Their hair was uniformly curly and stopped at the neck. Their ears were remarkably tiny. Their mouths were small, with bright red, thin lips. Their chins were pointed, their eyes large and mild.

They made no effort to communicate with me again, but simply stood around me smiling and making soft cooing

sounds to one another. I tried to engage them. I pointed to the Time Machine and to myself. Wanting to express the notion of time, I pointed to the sun. At once, a pretty little figure in checkered purple and white followed my gesture. He then astonished me by imitating the sound of thunder. He had asked, in fact, if I had come from the sun in a thunderstorm!

Were these creatures fools, I wondered? I had expected that the people of the distant future would be far ahead of us in knowledge. But from his response, it seemed to me that this creature was on the intellectual level of a small child. I felt disappointed, even cheated.

I nodded, pointed to the sun, and startled them with a vivid imitation of a thunderclap. They moved away from me and bowed. Then one of them came laughing toward me, carrying a chain of beautiful flowers that I had never seen

before. He put it around my neck. The others responded with applause. They were all delighted, and soon they were all gathering flowers and flinging them upon me. I was almost smothered with blossoms.

Then one suggested that their new plaything be exhibited in the nearest building. I was led past the White Sphinx toward a huge gray stone building. The Time Machine remained behind on the turf among the bushes.

We entered the stately building

through a huge doorway. My attention was drawn to the growing crowd of little people and the big, open doorway that yawned before me, shadowy and mysterious. My general impression of the world I saw over their heads was a tangled waste of beautiful bushes and flowers, long neglected and yet free of weeds.

The arch of the doorway was intricately carved. Several brightly dressed people met me in the doorway. We

entered together. I was in my dingy nine-teenth-century garments, and surround-ed by this swirling mass of colorful robes. I must have been a ridiculous sight!

The big doorway opened into a great hall. The walls were hung with dusty brown curtains, which covered win-dows of colored glass. The floor was made up of huge blocks of some very hard white metal. It was remarkably worn, the result, I supposed, of numerous generations of feet passing back and forth.

Tables made of slabs of polished stone, raised perhaps a foot from the floor, filled the room. Laid out upon these was a feast of fruits. Some of the strange fruits I recognized as massive forms of a raspberry or an orange. But for the most part they were unfamiliar.

Cushions were scattered between the tables. My hosts seated themselves on the cushions and gave me a sign to do the same. They then threw themselves into their feast, eating the fruit with their hands, flinging peels and stalks into round openings in the sides of the tables. I followed their example, for I felt thirsty and hungry. As I did so, I studied the hall at my leisure.

Perhaps what struck me most about my surroundings was their decay. The stained-glass windows were broken in many places. The curtains were covered with a thick coating of dust. The corner of the marble table near me was fractured. Nevertheless, the general effect was extremely rich and picturesque. There were a few hundred people dining in the hall. Most of them, seated as near to me as they could come, were watching me, their little eyes shining over the fruit they were eating.

These people of the remote future were strict vegetarians. While I was with them, my diet was limited to fruit as well. I later discovered that many

animals had become extinct. But the fruits were very delightful.

As soon as I satisfied my appetite, I resolved to learn the speech of these creatures. The fruits seemed a convenient thing to begin with. Holding one of them up, I began a series of sounds and gestures. I had considerable difficulty in getting my meaning across to them. At first my efforts met with surprised stares or laughter. But eventually a fair-haired little creature grasped my intention and said a word.

My first attempts to sound out the word caused a great amount of laughter. I felt like a schoolmaster among children. But I persisted until I knew a good number of nouns. It was slow work, and the little people soon tired. Their attention was easily diverted. So I was forced to let them give me lessons in small doses.

I quickly developed a low opinion of the little people's abilities. They were easily distracted and had very short attention spans.

It was evening when I left the great

hall. The scene was lit by the warm glow of the setting sun. Everything was so different from the world I had known. I decided to climb to the summit of a crest perhaps a mile and a half away. From there I could get a wider view of our planet as it presented itself in this year of Eight Hundred and Two Thousand, Seven Hundred and One.

As I walked, I looked for clues to explain the dilapidated condition in which I found the world. A little way up the hill, for instance, I saw a great heap of granite, bound together by masses of aluminum. It was a vast labyrinth of steep walls and crumpled ruins, overgrown with a mass of plant life. It was here that I was destined, at a later date, to have a very strange experience—the first hint of a still stranger discovery. But I will reveal that in due course.

I rested a while on a terrace. As I looked around I realized that there were no small houses to be seen. I concluded that the family unit must be extinct. These creatures must have taken up a communal way of life. The massive buildings that dotted the landscape were evidence of this.

Another odd thing was that it was hard to distinguish whether the little people were men or women. All of the things that mark off men from women in our day were absent. The long, flowing robes, plump limbs, hairless faces— these features blurred the boundaries between the sexes. The children seemed like miniature versions of the adults.

My attention was drawn to a pretty little structure, like a well under a domed roof. As I continued my stride upward I left my companions behind. I was alone for the first time. With a strange sense of freedom and adventure, I pushed on up to the crest.

There I found a seat of some yellow metal, corroded in places with pinkish rust and half-smothered in soft moss.

The armrests were carved to look like griffins' heads. I sat down on it and took in the broad view of the world under the sunset of that long day. It was as sweet and fair a view as I had ever seen. The Thames was visible below. The great palaces I spoke of stood among the greenery. Some were in ruins, and some were still occupied.

I believed that I had stumbled on humanity in its demise. It seemed a natural consequence of our own way of life. Strength is the outcome of need. The progress of civilization that makes life more and more comfortable had led to weakness. Man had finally triumphed over nature, and the harvest was what I saw!

Our current advances in science and medicine are small. The science of our time has attacked but a little of human disease. Gradually, we improve our favorite plants and animals by selective breeding. The result is that every now and then we have a new and better peach, a seedless grape, a sweeter and larger flower or a more desirable breed of cattle. We move slowly because our knowledge is limited. Someday all of these experiments will involve far less guesswork and yield far more impressive results. The whole world will be intelligent, educated, and cooperative. Nature will be conquered. In the end, wisely and carefully we will rearrange life to suit our human needs.

Over the course of many, many years, this process must have been done to perfection. The air was free from gnats, the earth from weeds or fungi, the fruits were sweet, and the flowers were delightful. Disease had been stamped out by many centuries of research and medical innovation. People found shelter in splendid palaces. Their clothing was quite elegant and comfortable. They had no need to work. I found no signs of shops or traffic, or of any of the many activities that fill our days. It was only natural on that golden evening that I would compare this wonderful new world to a paradise. I thought of the small, delicate stature of the people, their lack of intelligence, and those big, abundant ruins. Humanity had been strong, energetic, and intelligent and had used all of that vitality to change the conditions under which it lived to make them more comfortable. For such a life, what we

called the weak are as well equipped as the stong.

As I stood there thinking under the darkening sky, I thought I had figured it all out. I thought that I knew all there was to know about this new world. My explanation was very simple, and it was reasonable enough—as most wrong theories are!

# CHAPTER 5

# THE TIME MACHINE VANISHES

A full moon rose out of an overflow of silver light in the northeast. The bright little figures below disappeared, a noiseless owl flitted by. I shivered with the chill of the night. I decided to return and find a place to sleep.

I looked for the huge building in which we ate. Then my eye traveled along to the figure of the White Sphinx. I looked at the lawn. A chill ran through me. "No," I said to myself. "That was not the lawn." But it was the lawn. I was certain. The face of the White Sphinx looked toward it. You cannot imagine my panic as I realized that the Time Machine was gone!

I became frantic with the thought of being stranded in this strange place. I ran with great leaping strides down the slope. I kept reassuring myself, "They have moved it a little, pushed it under the bushes out of the way." Still, I ran with all my might. Instinctively, I knew that the machine was hidden from me. I cried out, but no one answered. Not a creature

seemed to be stirring in that moonlit world.

When I reached the lawn, my worst fears were realized: There was no trace of the Time Machine. I felt faint and cold. Above me towered the White Sphinx, glowing eerily in the light of the rising moon. Its smile seemed to mock me.

I knew that the little people were incapable of moving the machine. A new worry came over me. I had the sense

that there were other creatures or powers at work in this world. Yet, the fact that I still had the levers meant that the machine could not have traveled to another age. But then, where could it be?

I wildly ran in and out among the moonlit bushes all around the White Sphinx. Then, sobbing, I went down to the great building of stone. The big hall was dark, silent, and deserted. I slipped on the uneven floor and fell over one of the stone tables, nearly breaking my shin. I lit a match and went on past the dusty curtains.

I found a second great hall, the floor covered with cushions. A dozen or so of the little people were sleeping on them. Raving and waving a match in front of me, I called out, "Where is my Time Machine?" Some laughed, but most of them looked frightened. These gentle, trusting creatures had seemed not to know fear. Here I was reviving

that crippling emotion.

Abruptly, I blew out the match. Knocking over one of the creatures, I went blundering across the big dining hall again, out under the moonlight. At last, I lay down on the ground near the White Sphinx and cried. Then I slept.

When I awoke it was day again. My senses began to return. I could take stock of my situation.

"Suppose the worst has happened," I said to myself. "Suppose the machine is gone—perhaps destroyed. The best thing to do is to be calm and patient, to learn the ways of these people, and to collect materials to make a new machine." That was my only hope, but it was better than despair. And, after all, this was a beautiful and curious world.

If the Time Machine had been hidden, I must find its hiding place and recover it by force or cunning. I found a groove ripped in the ground. It was about midway between the base of the White Sphinx and the marks of my feet, where, on arrival, I had struggled with the overturned machine. There were

other signs: strange, narrow footprints made by a sloth-like creature. I followed the footprints to the bronze pedestal on which the Sphinx rested. It was ornately decorated with framed panels on either side. I tapped on the panels. The pedestal was hollow. There were no handles or keyholes. But possibly the panels, if they were doors, opened from within. My instincts confirmed what the footprints suggested. My Time Machine was inside that pedestal. But how did it get there?

I saw the heads of two little people coming through the bushes toward me. I smiled and called them to me. Pointing to the bronze pedestal, I tried to indicate my wish to open it. But at my first gesture, they became agitated.

I banged the bronze panels with my fists. I thought I heard something stir inside, a sound like a soft chuckling. Then I found a big pebble near the river and used it as a hammer until I had flattened a coil in the decorations. Some of the green rust came off in powdery flakes. At last, hot and tired, I sat down to watch the place. But I was too restless to watch for long.

I got up after a time and walked aimlessly through the bushes toward the hill. "Patience," I said to myself. "If you want your machine again, you must leave that White Sphinx alone. If they mean no harm, then you will get it back as soon as you can ask for it. Learn the ways of this world. In the end you will find clues to it all." Then, all at once, the humor of the situation poured over me. I had spent years in study and toil to get into the future age. Now I was anxious to get out as quickly as I could! I could not help laughing at myself.

As I walked through the palace, the little people avoided me. I was careful not to follow them. In the course of a day or two they seemed to have forgotten my outburst. I made what progress I could to learn their language. I also continued my explorations. Either I missed some subtle point, or their language was excessively simple—almost entirely made up of nouns and verbs. There seemed to be little use of symbolic language.

From every hill I climbed, I saw splendid buildings, endlessly varied in material and style, lush patches of evergreens and blossom-laden trees. Here and there water shone like silver. Beyond, the land rose into gently slop-

ing hills and faded into the peaceful sky.

I saw a number of the domed wells I mentioned. Some seemed to be quite deep. I sat by the sides of the wells and peered down into the darkness. I could see no gleam of water. A lighted match sparked no reflection. But in all of them I heard a thud-thud-thud, like the hum of some big engine.

Overall, I learned very little about the mechanisms by which life functioned in this place. Try to picture what a native,

fresh from Central Africa, might think of modern-day London. What tales would he take back to the natives of his home country? And how much could he make his friends believe? This will give you an idea of how wide was the gap between these creatures and me! The details of their daily existence remained hidden from my eyes.

Puzzling over my first impressions of an automatic civilization and a decaying humanity, I realized that these assumptions could not account for all of the things I observed. The palaces I had explored were mere living places, great dining halls, and sleeping apartments. I could find no machinery and no appliances of any kind. Yet these people were clothed in beautiful fabrics that must at times need repair. Somehow such things must be made, but the little people didn't seem to work at anything. There were no shops and workplaces in view. They spent all their time playing,

bathing in the river, eating fruit and sleeping.

Then, what about the Time Machine? Something or someone had hidden it in the base of the White Sphinx. Why? I was stumped. And what about the waterless wells and the flickering pillars? I was completely dumbfounded!

# CHAPTER 6
## WEENA

One day I made a friend. It happened that, as I was watching some of the little people bathing, one of them was seized with a cramp and began drifting downstream. The main current ran rather swiftly, but not too strongly for even a moderate swimmer. But none of the little people tried to rescue the poor creature. She was drowning before their eyes.

I slipped off my clothes and, wading into the water at a point lower down, I caught her and drew her safely to land. A little rubbing of the limbs soon

revived her. I was relieved to see that she was all right. I had by this point such a low opinion of her kind that I did not expect any gratitude from her. Happily, I was proven wrong and discovered a delightful companion.

This happened in the morning. In the afternoon, I met her again as I was returning from an exploration. She received me with cries of delight and presented me with a big garland of flowers. This made me quite happy, as I had been feeling very lonely. We were soon seated together in a little stone arbor, engaged in conversation, chiefly of smiles. The creature's friendliness affected me exactly as a child's might have done. We passed each other flowers. She kissed my hands. I did the same to hers. I found out that her name was Weena.

She wanted to be with me always, and followed me everywhere I went. It tugged at my heart to tire her out, and then, moving on, to hear her cry out. But I had to continue my explorations. Her distress when I left her was very great, and I believe I had as much trouble as comfort from her devotion. Nevertheless, she was a great relief to me in my isolation. I thought it was mere childish affection that made her cling to me. I did not know what pain I had inflicted upon her when I left her.

Weena also showed me that the little people could feel fear. She was fearless enough in the daylight. But she dreaded the coming of night. Any darkness or shadows filled her with dread. So that is why, I thought, the little people gathered together in the palaces after dark. I never found one outside, or one sleeping alone inside, after dark. Yet I still missed the deeper lesson of that fear. In spite of Weena's distress, I persisted in sleeping away from their groupings. Although it troubled her greatly, in the end she slept with her head pillowed on my arm.

It must have been the night before Weena's rescue that I was awakened about dawn. I had been having a bad dream. I woke suddenly with the feeling that some colorless animal had just rushed out of the room. I tried to fall asleep again, but I felt restless and uncomfortable. I went outside the palace, into the morning air.

The dying moonlight and the first blush of dawn were mingled in a ghostly

half-light. The bushes were inky black, and the ground a dull gray. The sky was gloomy. I thought I saw ghosts up on the hill. As I scanned the slope, I saw white figures appear and disappear. Twice I thought I saw a solitary white, ape-like creature running quickly up the hill. Once near the ruins I saw a group of them carrying some dark body. It seemed that they vanished among the bushes. But I doubted my eyes.

As the light of the day came on, I

scanned the horizon. The white figures were gone. "They must have been ghosts," I told myself. Little did I know that they were soon to occupy my mind in a deadly fashion.

The climate in this place was unusually hot. It may be that the sun was hotter, or perhaps the earth was nearer to the sun. One particularly hot morning, as I was seeking shelter from the heat in a massive ruin near the palace where I slept and ate, a

remarkable thing happened. Clambering among the heaps of masonry, I found a narrow gallery. Its end and side windows were blocked by fallen masses of stone. The gallery's darkness made a stark contrast to the blazing sunlight outside. I entered it and groped around. The change from light to darkness made spots of color swim before my eyes. Suddenly, I halted. A pair of eyes shone out of the darkness, watching me.

I clenched my hands and stared back into the eyes. I was afraid to turn. Then I remembered my conclusions about the security in which humanity appeared to be living in this world. And then I recalled the little people's terror of the dark. Drawing up my courage, I took a step and called out. I put out my hand and touched something soft. At once the eyes darted sideways, and something white ran past me. My heart leaped and thundered in my chest as I saw a queer little ape-like figure, its head held down as if in shame, running across the sunlit space behind me. It ran right into a block of granite and staggered aside. But it recovered quickly and in a moment was hidden in a black shadow beneath another pile of ruined masonry.

It ran too fast for me to get a clear look, but I am certain that it was a dull white color and had large watery gray eyes. Also, there were patches of downy hair on its head and down its

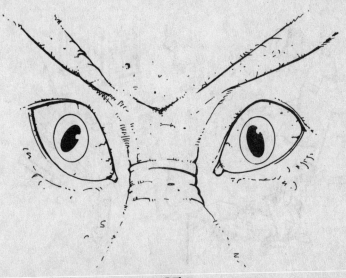

back. I cannot even say whether it ran on all fours, or only with its forearms held very low.

After a pause to collect myself, I followed the creature into the pile of ruins. I could not find it at first. But after a while, crawling around in the darkness, I came upon one of the wells. The opening was partially closed off by a fallen pillar. Could the creature have vanished down the shaft? I lit a match and looked down. I saw the small, white creature regarding me

steadily as it retreated. I shuddered. It clambered down the wall by means of a ladder down the shaft. Then the match burned my fingers and fell out of my hand, going out as it dropped. Quickly, I struck another one. But when the light flared, the creature was gone.

I sat peering down that well for a long while. I had a hard time persuading myself that the creature I had seen was human. But, gradually, a horrifying thought came to me. Humankind had not remained one species, but had differentiated into two distinct creatures. The graceful children of the daylight were not the sole descendants of our generation. This nocturnal animal I had discovered was also heir to all the ages.

It now seemed that the wells indicated something sinister underneath the calm, peaceful world of the little people. I sat on the edge of the well telling myself that there was nothing to fear, and that I must descend to the underworld for an answer. But I was afraid. As I hesitated, two of the beautiful little people came running playfully along in the sunshine.

They were troubled to find me peering down the well. When I pointed to the well and tried to question them about it, they became even more agitated. They turned away. As soon as I left them, I intended to go back to Weena and see what she could tell me. At least I now had a clue to the purpose of these wells, the ventilating towers, and the mystery of the ghosts.

Here is how my new theory ran. This second species of human lived underground. I had three reasons to convince me of this. In the first place, there was the bleached look common in most animals that live in the dark. Then, those large eyes, with their capacity for reflecting light, are common features of

nocturnal animals. And last of all, they were obviously confused in the sunlight.

Beneath my feet, then, the earth must be filled with huge tunnels, the habitat of this other race. The presence of ventilating shafts and wells along the hill slopes revealed the extent of this underground network. I assumed that the work being done to sustain the little people took place there.

I then turned my attention to discovering how the human race split in two directions. I dare say you will have no trouble coming to the same conclusion that I did. But like my other theories, this explanation fell far short of the truth.

At first, basing my ideas on our present-day situation, it seemed clear to me that the gradual widening of the gap between the men of business and the workers was the key to the mystery. There is a tendency to use underground space for the less attractive activities of

civilization. The number of underground activities increases daily. Evidently, this tendency had increased until all industry was housed underground. So, in the end, a vast network of tunnels had expanded into a world of its own.

Aboveground, one part of our race lived in pleasure and beauty. Belowground, the workers became more and more adapted to life underground. Those who best adapted would survive, while the others would not. The survivors would become as well adapted to the conditions of underground life, and as happy in their way, as the people living aboveground were to theirs. The weaknesses that were apparent in the little people, who lived aboveground, seemed a natural result of this train of events.

The too-perfect security of the little people had led them to a slow, steady degeneration. That, I could see clearly

enough. At this point, I still did not know what had happened to the creatures who lived underground. From what little I had seen of them, I could only imagine that the changes in form and way of life were even far more profound than among the little people. Through questioning the little people, I learned that the creatures feared by them were called the Morlocks. And the daylight creatures were called the Eloi.

Many doubts and more questions flooded my mind. Why had the Morlocks taken my Time Machine? For I was quite convinced that they had. And if the Eloi were masters, could they not return the machine to me? And why were the Eloi absolutely terrified of the dark?

Weena would not sit still long enough to listen to my questions. And when I pressed her, perhaps a little too harshly, she burst into tears. They were the only tears, except my own, that I ever saw in that place. Seeing her tears troubled me greatly. I did not want to upset her in any way. I turned my attention from the Morlocks and my many questions and concerns to cheering up my lovely companion. Before long, Weena was smiling and clapping her hands contentedly, while I solemnly burned a match before her.

CHAPTER 7
# THE MORLOCKS

It was two days before I continued my investigations. I felt a dread of the Morlocks. They were deathly cold to the touch. My fear was largely due to the influence of the Eloi, whose disgust of the Morlocks I now began to share.

The next night, I did not sleep well. My health may have been affected by the new environment and food. My mind was clouded with confusion and doubt. I felt nervous and apprehensive. It occurred to me that, in the course of a few days, the moon would pass through its last quarter. The nights would grow dark. The Morlocks would roam more freely aboveground.

In the back of my mind, I knew I was shirking an important duty. I was certain that the Time Machine was only to be recovered by boldly penetrating these underground mysteries. But I could not face the mystery. If I only had a companion it would have been different. But, aside from the child-like Eloi, I was horribly alone. The thought of climbing down into the darkness of the well terrified me.

And so my explorations continued in other directions. Going southwest I saw, far off, a vast green structure, much larger and different in character from any I knew of. The facade had an exotic look. The face of it had the sheen, as well as the pale green tint, of Chinese celadon porcelain. I wondered what the building was used for. But the day was growing late, and I had come upon the sight of the place after a long and tiring route. I told myself that I would explore further the following day, and I returned to a warm welcome from Weena.

But the next morning I saw that my interest in the Palace of Green Porcelain was yet another detour from solving the mystery of the Morlocks and retrieving my Time Machine. I decided then that I would make the descent immediately. In the early morning I started toward a

well near the ruins of granite and aluminum.

Weena ran with me. She danced beside me to the well, but when she saw me lean over the mouth and look down the shaft, she became alarmed. "Goodbye, Little Weena," I said, kissing her. Then I began to feel over the parapet for the climbing hooks. At first Weena watched me in amazement. Then she gave a most piteous cry. Running to

me, she began to pull at me with her little hands. I shook her off, perhaps a little roughly. In another moment I was in the throat of the well. I saw her agonized face over the edge and smiled to reassure her. Then I turned my attention to the unstable hooks to which I clung.

I had to climb down a shaft of perhaps two hundred yards. I was soon cramped and fatigued. One of the bars bent suddenly under my weight and almost swung me off into the darkness beneath. For a moment I hung by one hand.

After that experience I did not dare rest again. Though my arms and back were acutely painful, I went on climbing down the steep walls as quickly as possible. Glancing up, I saw the opening, now a small blue disk in which a star was visible. Weena's head appeared as a small black shadow. The thudding sound of a machine below grew louder. Everything except that little shape above was deep darkness. When I looked up again, Weena had disappeared.

I thought of trying to go back up the shaft, but even while I considered this, I continued to descend. At last, with intense relief, I saw a slender loophole in the wall. Crawling in, I found that it opened onto a narrow tunnel. There I could lie down and rest. My arms ached, my back was cramped, and my eyes burned. All around me, the air was full of the throb and hum of machinery pumping air down the shaft.

I do not know how long I lay there. At some point, I felt a soft hand touching my face. Starting up in the darkness, I fumbled for my matches. Hastily striking one, I saw three stooping white creatures similar to the one I had seen aboveground in the ruin. They retreated as the flame flickered and gave light. Living, as they did, in

this impenetrable darkness, their eyes were abnormally large and sensitive. I have no doubt that they could see me. They did not seem to have any fear of me, but as soon as I struck a match, they fled. Their eyes glared at me from the dark tunnels.

I called out to them in the Elois' language. But the language they spoke must have been different from that of the Eloi. As I felt my way along the tunnel, I found that the noise of

machinery grew louder. I came to a large open space. Striking another match, I saw that I had entered a vast, arched cavern, which stretched into utter darkness beyond the range of my light.

The atmosphere was very stuffy and oppressive. The scent of freshly shed blood filled the air. Some way down stood a little table of white metal, laid with what seemed to be a meal. The Morlocks were not vegetarians!

I have thought since how unprepared I was for such an experience. When I had started to work on the Time Machine, I made the absurd assumption that the race of the future would certainly be infinitely ahead of us in all their appliances. I had come without arms, without medicine—even without enough matches. If only I had thought of a camera! I could have flashed that glimpse of the underworld in a second and retreated to examine it in safety.

But, as it was, I stood there with only my own hands and the four matches that still remained in my supply.

While I stood in the dark, a hand touched mine. Limp fingers felt over my face, and I smelled an unpleasant odor. I imagined that I heard the breathing of a crowd of those dreadful Morlocks surrounding me. Hands behind me plucked at my clothing. The sense of these unseen creatures examining me was unnerving. I shouted at them as loudly as I could. They moved away. But then I felt them approaching me again. They clutched at me more boldly, whispering muffled sounds to one another. I shivered violently and shouted again. This time they were not so seriously alarmed. They made a queer laughing noise as they came back at me. I tried to strike another match and escape under the protection of its glare. I did so and, eeking out the flicker with a scrap of paper from my pocket, I hurried back to the narrow tunnel. But I had hardly entered when my light was blown out. In the all-consuming

darkness, I heard the Morlocks rustling like wind through the trees and pattering like the rain as they hurried after me.

Several hands clutched at me, trying to haul me back. I struck another light and waved it in their dazzled faces. They were a ghastly sight as they stared in their blindness and bewilderment. I retreated again. When my second match had burned out, I struck my third. It had almost burned through when I

reached the opening into the shaft. I lay down on the edge, for the throb of the great pump below made me light-headed. Then I felt sideways for the metal hooks. As I did so, my feet were grasped from behind. I was violently tugged backward. I lit my last match and it sputtered out! But I had my hand on the hooks now and, kicking violently, I pulled myself away from the Morlocks' clutches. I raced up the shaft while they stayed peering and blinking up at me.

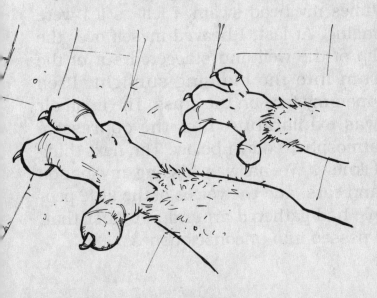

In the last stretches of my climb, a crippling nausea came over me. Several times my head swam. I felt as if I were falling. At last, I heaved myself over the lip of the well and staggered out of the ruin into the blinding sunlight. I fell upon my face on the grass. The fresh air was exhilarating after the oppressive atmosphere down below. The next thing I knew, Weena was kissing my hands and ears, and the voices of the little people had gathered around me. After that, I passed into unconsciousness.

## CHAPTER 8
# A CHILLING DISCOVERY

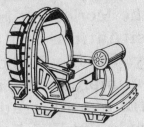

Now, indeed, my plight seemed worse than before. There was an entirely new element evident in the Morlocks, something inhuman and evil. I felt like a beast in a trap, whose enemy would pounce without warning.

With the approaching darkness of the new moon, my worries increased. Each night there was a longer interval of darkness. And I now understood the reason for the Elois' fear of the dark. What horrible evil did the Morlocks do under the new moon?

I felt pretty sure now that my second theory was completely wrong. The Eloi might once have been the favored class and the Morlocks their servants. But that situation had long since passed away. The Eloi had decayed to a beautiful but unproductive race. Out of habit of time and tradition, the Morlocks made the Elois' clothing and performed all the necessary services of existence. But, clearly, the Eloi were terrified of their servants. At that moment, the very large piece of meat that I had seen underground came to

mind. The memory reinforced my belief in a more sinister connection between the Morlocks and the beautiful little people.

The Eloi might be paralyzed by their fear, but I was a different breed. I determined to make myself arms and to find a safe place to sleep. With that refuge as a base, I could face this strange world with some of the confidence I had lost. I felt I could never sleep again until my bed was secure from the Morlocks.

During the afternoon, I wandered along the valley of the Thames, looking for a place that was beyond the reach of the Morlocks, who were skilled climbers. All the buildings and trees in my view would be easily accessible to them. Then I thought of the tall pinnacles of the Palace of Green Porcelain and the polished gleam of its walls.

That evening, I took Weena like a child upon my shoulder and went up the hills toward the southwest. I had difficulty making the long journey because the heel of one of my shoes was loose and a nail was working through the sole. I had not thought to wear sturdy shoes on my journey. Being quite lame by that point, I didn't reach the palace until well after sunset.

Weena continued to amuse me. She ran beside me until some flowers caught her attention. Then she plucked a few and stuck them in my pockets. That reminds me! Look what I found while I

was changing my clothes!

*The Time Traveler paused and put his hand into his pocket, He silently placed two very large white blossoms, clearly past their prime, on the table. Then he continued his amazing tale.*

Eventually, though, Weena tired and wanted to return home. I did my best to console her. But I was well aware of the dangers of the darkness. As evening fell, I imagined that I could feel the hollowness of the ground beneath my feet.

I feared that the Morlocks were waiting for the dark in order to pounce on us.

I took Weena in my arms and soothed her. Then, as the darkness grew deeper, she put her arms around my neck. Closing her eyes, she tightly pressed her face against my shoulder. We went down a long slope into a valley, and there in the dimness I almost stumbled into a little river. I waded in and went up the opposite side of the valley, past a number of houses. I saw a statue that resembled a headless faun and clusters of acacia trees. There was no trace of the Morlocks, but the darker hours were still to come.

From the top of the next hill I saw a thick wood spreading wide and black before me. To enter this vast darkness caused me no little worry, but I was tired. I set Weena down and tried to decide what to do next. The Palace of Green Porcelain, which had served as my compass, was no longer in view, so I no longer had my bearings. What might this wood hide in its dark shadows? And even if there were no Morlocks, I was certain that the tangled branches and stumps would be dangerous in themselves. Thus, I chose the open hill as the safest place for us to sleep.

Weena had fallen asleep. I wrapped her in my jacket. I sat down beside her to wait for the moon to rise. The hill was quiet and deserted, but I could hear strange stirrings coming from the direction of the wood. The brightness of the stars proved a great comfort. The constellations seemed to have rearranged themselves over the course of time, but I thought I could still recognize the Milky Way.

Looking at the great expanse of sky and the stars, so far away, my own cares seemed small, even trivial. All of man's great aspirations, all of the languages, traditions, organizations–all had been swept away over the course of time. All that was left were these two races and the remains of a crumpled society.

Then I thought of the intense fear that hovered like a tangible presence between the Eloi and the Morlocks. I shivered, thinking of the meat that nourished the Morlocks. It was too horrible! I looked at little Weena sleeping beside me, her face white and gentle under the stars. I pushed away the thought.

I fought to keep my mind off the

Morlocks as the long night wore on. The sky remained very clear, except for a hazy cloud passing by now and then. I must have dozed off occasionally. Then my watch came to an end as the sun began to rise in the east. I was, indeed, thankful that no Morlocks had troubled us. The dawning of a new day fired up my courage. When I stood up, my swollen foot hurt terribly, so I flung off my shoes, which had become useless to me by that time.

I awakened Weena, and we went

down into the woods. In the daylight, it was warm and welcoming. We easily found some fruit for breakfast. We soon met more of the Eloi, who laughed and danced in the sunlight as though there had never been anything to fear. Their careless abandon reminded me of the meat I had seen in the underworld. Could it be that these lovely creatures were destined to a miserable fate? Food must have run short; and in the past, men have resorted to eating human

flesh. After all, these hideous creatures were less human and more remote than our cannibal ancestors of thousands of years ago. The Eloi were terrified of the dark, but could they understand their awful fate? To me, at least, they didn't seem to have the intelligence to grasp its true import.

I abandoned these gloomy thoughts and turned my attention to finding a safe place and making some weapons to defend myself against the Morlocks.

Since the Morlocks were afraid of light, I knew I must find a source of fire to make a torch, in case my other weapons failed. I also needed to find something capable of smashing open the bronze doors under the White Sphinx. I had in mind a battering ram. I would break into my machine's hiding place, leading the way with my torch to frighten away my enemies. With my machine back under my control, I could escape. I had grown very fond of Weena so I resolved to take her home with me. These plans gave me hope. I proceeded toward the place that I believed would be a safe haven from the Morlocks.

# CHAPTER 9
# THE PALACE OF
# GREEN PORCELAIN

We came to the Palace of Green Porcelain at about midday. It was a wreck of a thing, long fallen into ruin. Only a bit of glass remained in its windows, and great sheets of the green facing had fallen away from the corroded metallic framework. The building topped a grassy slope. To the northeast I saw a large creek.

I confirmed in my examination of the building that the palace was, indeed, made of porcelain. A message, written in letters I could not read, was written across its face. I turned to

Weena for some help, but the writing wasn't at all familiar to her.

The doors were broken, and we were able to walk right into a long gallery lit by many side windows. A thick coating of dust covered the tiled floors. As in a museum, there were objects on display all around the gallery. They, too, were covered in dust. A huge dinosaur skeleton took center stage in the middle of the hall. On shelves along the sides, I found some airtight specimen cases. Their contents were fairly well preserved.

The silence of this grand showplace was eerie. The piles of dust quieted even our footsteps. Weena entertained herself by rolling a sea urchin down the sloping glass of a case. When she tired of that, she came over, very quietly took my hand, and stood beside me.

Next we found another short gallery running diagonally to the first. It contained minerals. When I saw a block of

sulfur, my mind turned to gunpowder. But I could find nothing with which to ignite it. I went on to another section, which was devoted to natural history. But its contents had deteriorated.

Then we came to an immense and poorly lit gallery. At intervals, white globes hung down from the ceiling, many of them cracked and smashed. I was excited to see the huge forms of big machines. Most were as dilapidated as the rest of the building. But some were more or less intact. I found some delight in guessing what the machines had been used for.

Weena's sudden reappearance at my side startled me. She alerted me to the dangerously sloping floor in this gallery. The place where I had come in was quite aboveground and was lit by narrow windows, like slits in the wall. But as we went down the length, the ground came up against these windows, until at last there was a pit and only a narrow line of daylight at the top. I had been too absorbed in my game to notice the gradual dimming of light. Now I saw that the gallery ran down into deep darkness. I saw that the dust here was less abundant.

A number of small, narrow footprints imprinted the dust. I became alarmed that it was already late in the afternoon. I was still without the three things I had felt were necessary to my survival: a safe resting place, weapons, and a source of fire. These fears were

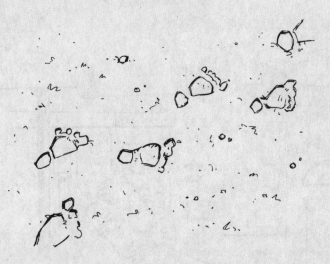

punctuated by the alarming sounds of pattering feet and the cooing noises I had heard down the well.

I let go of Weena's hand and turned to one of the machines. It had a lever similar to those in a signal-box. I jumped up on it and grasped the lever in my hands, putting all of my weight upon it sideways. Weena was deserted in the central aisle. She began to whimper. I had judged the strength of the lever pretty well, for it snapped after a minute's strain. I turned toward Weena

with an iron bar in my hand more than sufficient for any Morlock skull.

With the iron bar in one hand and Weena in the other, I went out of that gallery and into another, still larger one. It reminded me of a military chapel hung with tattered flags. I realized that the brown and charred rags that hung from the sides of it were the decayed remains of books. Here and there, warped boards and cracked metallic clasps appeared to confirm my suspicion.

A broad staircase then took us to a gallery of chemistry. Except at one end where the roof had collapsed, this gallery was well preserved. I hoped to find something useful to me here. And at last, in one of the airtight cases, I found a box of matches. They were not even damp. I now had a powerful weapon to use against the Morlocks. I was so happy at this discovery that I danced along with Weena.

Although this discovery was unlikely, I found a far unlikelier substance. A bit of camphor was preserved in a sealed jar. In the universal decay around me, this volatile substance had survived, perhaps through many thousands of centuries! I was about to throw it away, but I remembered that it burned with a steady, bright flame. I put it in my pocket, intending to use it as a candle. Though I looked quite carefully, I did not find any explosives with which to break through the bronze doors.

There were many curious objects in this strange museum. In one gallery I found rusting stands of weapons and armor and was tempted to take a hatchet or a sword. I could not carry both, however, and my iron bar seemed an able tool to use against the bronze doors.

In another place was a vast array of idols—Polynesian, Mexican, Grecian,

Phoenician and one from almost every other country on earth. I gave in to an irresistible impulse to write my name upon the nose of an ancient stone-carved monster from South America.

Moving on, we came to a little open court within the palace. It was lush and green, with three lovely fruit trees. We rested on the open grass and refreshed ourselves. Our rest was brief though, because night was creeping upon us. I still needed to find a place secure against my enemies. Luckily I now had

in my possession a thing that was, perhaps, the best defense against the Morlocks—I had matches! I had the camphor in my pocket, too, if a blaze were needed. It occurred to me that we might pass the night out in the open, protected by the light from a fire. In the morning, I could turn all of my attention to getting my machine back.

# CHAPTER 10

# FIRE!

We left the palace while the sun was still partly above the horizon. I was determined to reach the White Sphinx early the next morning. My plan was to go as far as possible that night and then build a fire to sleep in the protection of its glare. As we traveled, I gathered sticks and dried grass for the fire. With this load, our progress was slower than I had hoped for.

Both Weena and I were tired, as well, which slowed us down. It was night before we reached the woods. Fearing the darkness of the woods, Weena wanted to stop. But an unshakable sense of dread drove me onward. I had been without sleep for a night and two days. I was feverish and irritable. I felt sleep coming upon me, and the Morlocks with it.

My fears were soon confirmed. In the black bushes behind us, I saw three crouching figures. In the darkness, with the long grass and bushes surrounding us, I was worried about being taken by surprise. The forest, I calculated, was less than a mile across. If we could get through it to the open hillside, I felt we would have greater protection.

With the matches and camphor, I could light our path through the woods. But I would not be able to do so and carry the firewood. Then I thought of how amazed the Morlocks would be by a grand demonstration. What seemed a great idea proved to be disastrous, as you will soon hear.

To Weena, and I suppose to the

Morlocks, the red tongues of fire that went licking up my heap of wood were a new experience—delightful to one, and terrifying to the other.

Weena wanted to run to it and play with it. I worried that she would jump right into the flames. I picked her up and ran boldly for the woods. For a little way the glare of the fire lit our path. Looking back, I could see, through the dangled growth, that from my heap of sticks the blaze had spread to some bushes. A curved line of fire was creep-

ing up the grass of the hill. I laughed and turned again to the dark trees before me. Upon my left arm I carried Weena; in my right hand I had my iron bar.

For some way, the only sound I heard was the crackling twigs under my feet, the faint rustle of the breeze above, my own breathing and the throb of my heart beating. But then I heard that strange pattering I now associated with the Morlocks. I pushed on grimly. The pattering grew closer, and cooing voices joined it. There were evidently several Morlocks. They were gaining on us. I felt a tug at my coat, then something at my arm. Weena shivered violently and then became still.

I put her down to get a match. While I fumbled in my pockets, a struggle began in the darkness about my knees. Soft little hands crept over my coat and back and touched my

neck. Then the match scratched and fizzed. I held it out and saw the white backs of the Morlocks fleeing through the trees. I took a lump of camphor from my pocket and prepared to light it when the match burned down. Weena was lying on the ground, clutching my feet but otherwise motionless. I lit the block of camphor and flung it to the ground. It split and flared up, driving back the Morlocks and the shadows.

I knelt down and lifted Weena. She had fainted. I put her carefully upon my shoulder and rose to push on. But now I had lost our path. For all I knew, I might be facing back toward the Palace of Green Porcelain. The only thing to do was build a fire and make a camp until the daylight came to make our way clear. As I collected sticks and leaves, the Morlocks' eyes shone eerily out of the shadows around us.

The camphor flickered and went out. Lighting another match, I saw that some of the Morlocks had been approaching Weena. One was so blinded by the light that he came straight for me. I felt his bones grind under the blow of my fist. He staggered a little way and then fell to the ground. I lit another piece of camphor and continued to gather materials for my bonfire. I noticed some dry foliage above me. Since my arrival on the Time Machine, a week ago, no rain had fallen. So instead of searching among the trees for fallen twigs, I began leaping up and dragging down dry branches. Very soon I had a choking fire of green wood and dry sticks. Then I turned to where Weena lay beside my iron bar. I tried to revive her, but she lay perfectly still.

My fire would not need stoking for an hour or so. I felt very weary and sat down to rest. I seemed just to nod off for a bit. But when I opened my eyes it was dark and the Morlocks had their

hands upon me. Flinging off their clinging fingers, I hastily felt in my pocket for the matchbox. It was gone! Then the fiends were at me again. In the tussle, I realized I had fallen asleep and my fire had gone out. The air was full of the smell of burning wood. I was caught by the neck, by the hair, by the arms, and was pulled down. I felt as if I were in a monstrous spider's web. The Morlocks overpowered me, and I fell to the ground. Their little teeth nipped at my neck. I rolled over. As I

did so, my hand felt my iron bar. I struggled up, shaking the Morlocks off of me. Holding the bar short, I thrust it out toward their faces. I hit my target and, in a moment, I was free.

Although I believed that both Weena and I were lost, I wanted to make the Morlocks pay for how they had terrorized the Eloi and me. I stood with my back to a tree, swinging the iron bar before me. The wood echoed with the stir and cries of Morlocks. A minute passed. The din became a dull roar.

Yet none came within reach. I stood glaring into the pitch dark. What if the Morlocks were afraid? This possibility revived my hope. Then the darkness was lit by a strange glow. Very dimly, I began to see the Morlocks crowding about me—three battered at my feet.

Others were running in a never-ending stream from behind me and away through the wood in front. Their backs had a reddish tint. I stood with my mouth open as I saw a red spark go drifting across a gap of starlight between the branches and vanish. The smell of burning wood, the low murmur that was growing into a gusty roar, the red glow, the Morlocks' flight—it could only mean one thing. Fire!

Stepping out from behind my tree and looking back, I saw flames darting through the burning forest. My bonfire had exploded into this raging fury. I looked for Weena, but she was gone.

The quick advance of the fire left me little time to plan my next move. Gripping the iron bar, I followed in the Morlocks' path. It was a close race. The flame once crept forward so swiftly on my right as I ran that I was outflanked and had to strike off to the left. But at last I came to a small open space. A Morlock came blundering toward me, then past me, and went on straight into the fire!

And now I will tell you the most horrible thing I encountered in that future age. The wood and hillside were as bright as day with the reflection of the

fire. In the center was a small rise, crowned by a scorched hawthorn. Beyond this was another arm of the burning forest, with yellow tongues leaping and dancing from it, completely encircling the space with a fence of fire. On the hillside, Morlocks were dazzled by the light and heat. They ran here and there against one another in their bewilderment.

Although they were quite blinded by the light, I struck furiously at them with my bar, in a frenzy of fear, as they approached me. I killed one and crippled several more. But when I had watched the gestures of one of them groping under the hawthorn against the red sky, and heard their moans, I was assured of their absolute helplessness and misery. I gave up the fight.

Every now and then one would come straight toward me, awakening the sense of dread that I seemed to carry with me during my time in this future world. At one point, the flames died down and I worried that the demons would be able to see me. Luckily, the fire burst out again. I was not forced to defend myself. I walked carefully around the hill, looking for some sign of Weena. But she was gone.

Exhausted, I sat down on the summit of the hill and watched this incredible sight. A company of blind creatures groped aimlessly, crying out to one another, as the glare and heat of the fire tortured them. Coils of smoke streamed across the sky. Occasionally, the thick band broke and little stars peaked through, remote as though they belonged to another universe. A few of the Morlocks came blundering into me. I drove them off with blows of my fists, trembling as I did so.

It seemed like a nightmare to me. I bit myself and screamed to make sure I was awake. I beat the ground with my

hands, got up, and sat down again, wandered here and there, and again sat down. I cannot describe the horror I felt as I saw Morlocks put their heads down in agony and rush into the flames. But, at last, above the diminishing glow of the fire, above the streaming clouds of black smoke and the charred tree stumps, daylight mercifully appeared.

I searched again for Weena, but in vain. The Morlocks must have abandoned her little body in the forest. Knowing that Weena had not provided

meat for these creatures was a great relief.

The hill I stood upon was like an island in the forest. From the top, through a haze of smoke, I saw the Palace of Green Porcelain. Now I could get my bearings and head in the direction of the White Sphinx. Leaving this scene of death and destruction, I tied some grass around my feet and limped through smoking ashes and blackened stems. Weena's loss left me once again utterly alone, and weighed heavily on me. Now, in this old familiar room, it is more like the sorrow of a dream than an actual loss. Thoughts of my home and my friends came rushing over me. How I longed to return to you all!

As I walked over the smoking ashes under the bright morning sky, I discovered in my trouser pockets some loose matches! The box must have leaked before it was lost. Relieved, I moved on to reclaim my machine.

CHAPTER 11

# AMBUSHED

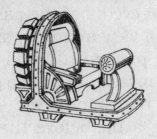

At about eight or nine o'clock that morning I came to the same seat of yellow metal from which I had viewed the world upon the evening of my arrival. I thought of the judgments I had made that evening concerning this world, and laughed bitterly. I now saw the same stately palaces, lush foliage, sparkling rivers, the cheerfully dressed little people—but it all seemed different. And like stains upon the landscape, the domed wells marked the entrances to the Morlocks' abode. The picture was disjointed—a beautiful paradise covering over a hellish underworld.

After the events of the past few days, the tranquil view and the warm sunlight were very pleasant. I was very tired. Spreading myself out on the grass, I had a long and refreshing sleep.

I awoke a bit before the sun set. I now felt safe against the Morlocks. Stretching myself, I walked down the hill toward the White Sphinx. I had my iron bar in one hand. The other hand played with the matches in my pocket.

You can imagine my shock as I

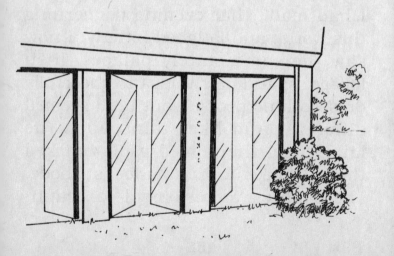

approached the base of the White Sphinx and found that the bronze doors stood open. I stopped short before them, hesitating to enter. Inside, I saw a small compartment. The Time Machine rested on a raised area in the corner. I felt for the levers in my pocket. So here, after all my plans for breaking into the White Sphinx, the Morlocks offered a meek surrender. I threw my iron bar away.

As I stooped to enter, an idea, like a light, came into my mind. For once, at least, I grasped the intentions of the Morlocks. I stepped through the bronze frame and up to the Time Machine. I was surprised to find it had been carefully oiled and cleaned. The Morlocks may have even partially taken it apart, trying to understand its mechanism.

Now as I stood and examined my machine, the danger I had feared all along came to be. The bronze panels suddenly slid up and shut with a clang. I was trapped. Or so the Morlocks thought. I chuckled gleefully.

I could hear their murmuring laughter as they came toward me. Very calmly, I tried to strike a match. I had only to attach the levers and depart like a ghost. But I had overlooked one little thing: These matches were the type that light only on the box!

The brutes were close upon me. One touched me. I made a sweeping blow in the dark at them with the levers. I began to scramble into the saddle of the machine. Then came one hand upon me and then another. I fought against

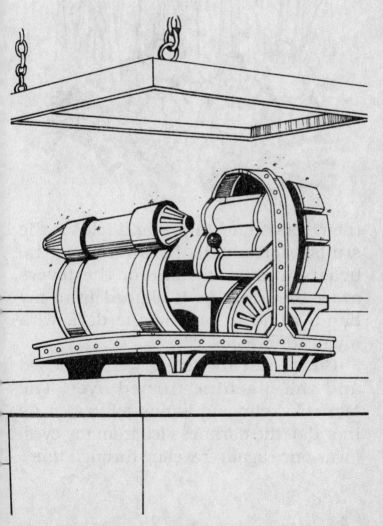

their persistent fingers and felt for the studs over which the levers fit. The beasts almost got one of the levers away from me. As it slipped from my hand, I had to butt in the dark with my head to recover it.

But at last the levers were attached and the machine turned over. The Morlocks' clinging hands fell away. As they did, the darkness fell from my eyes. I was once again traveling through time.

# CHAPTER 12
## A DETOUR

I have already described the dizzying effects of traveling through time. Adding to my distress, this time I was seated incorrectly in the saddle. Lacking stability, I clung to the machine as it swayed and vibrated. When I was able to look at the dials, I was amazed to find where I had arrived. Instead of reversing the levers, I had made the machine go forward even farther into the future!

As I drove on, the pulsating grayness grew darker. Although I was still traveling at great speed, the blinking succession of day and night, which usually indicated a slower pace, returned and grew more and more pronounced. I was puzzled. The alternations of night and day grew slower and slower. So did the passage of the sun across the sky. At last a steady twilight brooded over the earth, broken now and then when a comet glared across the darkening sky. The band of light indicating the sun had long since disappeared. The sun had ceased to set and simply rose and fell in the west, growing redder and broader.

There was no sign of the moon. The stars no longer circled about and became creeping points of light.

Some time before I stopped, the sun, red and very large, sat still upon the horizon. The earth had come to rest with one face to the sun, as even in our own time the moon faces the earth. To prevent another headlong fall, I cautiously began to reverse the motion. The hands on the dials slowed until the thousands hand was still and the one for each day was slow enough to read.

As they did so, I saw the dim outlines of a deserted beach.

I stopped very gently and looked around. To the northeast, the sky was inky black, punctuated by the steady glow of stars. Overhead, it was bloodred and starless. To the southeast, the sky grew brighter to a glowing scarlet. In this direction, cut by the horizon, lay the huge hull of the sun, red and motionless. The only signs of life were patches of intensely green vegetation covering the ground. It was the same rich green of forest moss, which also

grows in a perpetual twilight.

The machine had landed on a sloping beach. Everything was utterly still—no wind and no waves broke the eerily tranquil atmosphere. Only a slight oily swell rose and fell like gentle breathing on the water's surface. A thick crust of salt marked the water's edge. It hurt to breathe, as in mountainous areas where the air is thin.

I heard a scream pierce the silence. Looking up the slope, I saw a huge white creature, similar to a butterfly, flutter up into the sky and disappear over some low hills. Something moved and caught my eye. What I had thought was a reddish mass of rock was, in fact, a huge crab-like monster. The sight of its many legs, swaying claws, and long antennae froze me on the spot. I felt a tickling on my cheek as though a fly had landed there. I tried to brush it away with my hand. But in a moment it returned. Almost immediately, another

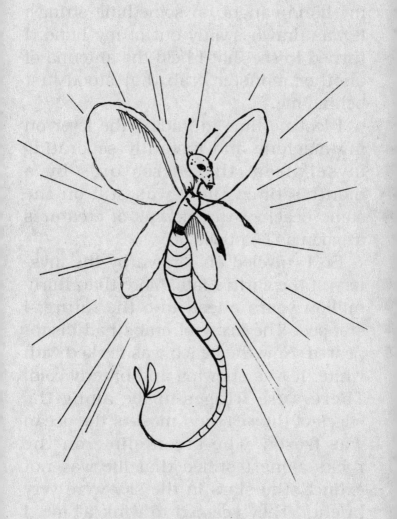

came by my ear. I tried to fling it off, and my hand caught on something stringy. It was drawn swiftly out of my hand. I turned to see that I held the antenna of another monster crab that stood just behind me.

I lost no time in finding the lever on my machine and instantly separating myself from these creatures by a month's time. But I was still on the same beach. I saw dozens of creatures as soon as I stopped.

So I traveled on, drawn by the mystery of the earth's fate. More than thirty million years ahead into the future, I stopped. The army of crabs had disappeared. Now the beach was flecked with white. It was snowing and bitterly cold. There were fringes of ice along the edges of the sea, and most of the ocean was frozen. The green slime on the rocks alone testified that life was not extinct. The stars in the sky were very bright. They seemed to wink at me. I

thought some dark object moved on the sandbank, but I told myself that my eyes had deceived me.

Suddenly, I noticed that the sun had changed. An eclipse was beginning. As the darkness grew, a cold wind began to blow from the east. The snowfall became heavier. At last, one by one, the white peaks of the distant hills vanished into the darkness. The breeze rose to a moaning wind. I saw the central shadow of the eclipse sweeping toward me. Then all was black.

I felt sick and would have fallen but, like an answered prayer, the edge of the sun reappeared. I dismounted the machine to recover myself. As I stood sick and confused, I saw again the moving thing on the sandbank. It was round, perhaps the size of a football, with tentacles spreading out from its frame. I thought I would faint. But I fought to stay conscious. I scrambled back onto the machine.

# CHAPTER 13
# A SAFE RETURN

I felt a great sense of relief as the hands spun backward on the dials. At last I saw again the dim shadows of houses. When the millions dial was at zero, I decreased my speed. The thousands hand ran back to the starting point, and the familiar walls of my laboratory came into view. Very gently, I came to a stop.

As I mentioned at the start of my tale, when I began my travels upon the Time Machine I saw my housekeeper walk across the room, traveling at the speed of a rocket. On my return, I again passed through that moment when she crossed the laboratory. I witnessed an exact inversion of the previous course of events. The door at the lower end opened. She walked up the laboratory backward and disappeared behind the door by which she had previously entered.

At this point I stopped the machine. I happily set my eyes on the laboratory just as I had left it. I raised myself, shakily, off the machine and sat on the bench. I blinked my eyes. Had it

all been a dream?

No! It couldn't have been. The machine had been at the southeast corner of the laboratory and it had landed in the northwest corner. That gives you the exact distance from the lawn to the base of the White Sphinx!

I steadied myself, rose from the bench, and came through the hallway. The newspaper on the table by the door told me that the date was indeed today, and the clock said the time was

nearly eight o'clock. I heard your voices and the clatter of plates. The smell of food restored my spirits. You know the rest. I washed and dined. I am telling you my story.

\* \* \* \* \* \* \* \* \* \* \* \* \* \*

The Time Traveler shook his head and looked at the faces around him. "No," he said. "I cannot expect you to believe it. Taking it as a story, what do you think of my tale?"

There was a momentary stillness. Then chairs began to creak and shoes to scrape upon the carpet. I looked around at our company. The doctor was closely studying our host. The Editor was staring at the end of his cigar. The Journalist reached for his watch. No one else moved.

The Editor stood up. He said, "What a pity it is that you're not a writer of stories!"

The Time Traveler turned to us. "To tell you the truth," he said, "I hardly

believe it myself."

He looked again at the withered white flowers he had placed on the table. Then he turned over one hand. I saw that he was looking at some half-healed scars on his knuckles.

The Doctor rose, came to the lamp, and examined the flowers. "Strange," he murmured. The Psychologist leaned forward to examine them, holding out his hand for a specimen.

"I would like to study these," said the Doctor. "I've never seen anything like them. May I have them?"

The Time Traveler hesitated.

"Certainly not," he answered.

"Where did you get them, really?" asked the Doctor.

"From Weena, when I traveled into Time." He stared around the room and asked, "Did I ever make a Time Machine? They say life is a dream, a precious, poor dream, at times, but this one is madness. I must look at that machine, if there is one!"

He took the lamp and carried it into the hallway. We followed him. There in the flickering light of the lamp was the machine, sure enough, a curiosity of brass, ebony, ivory, and quartz. It was covered with dirt and bits of grass and moss, and one of the rails was bent.

The Time Traveler put the lamp down on the bench. He ran his hand along the damaged rail. "The story I told you was true," he announced. He led us back into the other room.

It was now early morning. As we prepared to leave, the Time Traveler came into the hall and helped the Editor put on his coat. The Doctor told him he was suffering from overwork. He just laughed and wished us all a good night.

Although I was desperately in need of rest, I spent most of the night thinking about his story. The next day, I went to see the Time Traveler again. His house-keeper said he was in the laboratory. But it was empty. I stared for a minute at the Time Machine. I put out my hand

and touched the lever. It swayed like a bough shaken by the wind. I felt as a child does when he gets into something forbidden.

I walked back through the hall and found my friend in the drawing room. He had a small camera in his hand and a knapsack on his shoulder. He laughed when he saw me.

He said, "I'm very busy with that thing in there."

"But is it not some hoax?" I asked. "Do you really travel through time?"

"Really and truly I do," he replied. "If you'll stay for lunch, I'll prove it to you. But I need half an hour."

I agreed to stay, and off he went to his laboratory. I heard the door slam. I sat down to read the paper. I remembered that I had promised to meet someone at two o'clock. I looked at my watch. I could barely get there by two. I went down the hallway to tell the Time Traveler that I could not wait.

As I reached for the doorknob, I heard a cry and then a click and a thud. A gust of air swirled around me when I opened the door. I heard the sound of broken glass falling on the floor. The room was empty! I saw a ghostly figure sitting in a whirling mass of glitter and brass. Visible through the figure, I saw quite clearly the bench behind it with its sheets of drawings. I rubbed my eyes and blinked. The Time Machine had disappeared. The space it had occupied was empty. A pane of the skylight had blown in. As I stood staring, the door into the garden opened, and one of the servants appeared.

"Has he gone out that way?" I asked.

"No, sir. No one has come out this way. I was expecting to find him here," the servant said.

I decided to skip my appointment and wait for the Time Traveler to return. But I am beginning to fear that I must wait a lifetime. The Time Traveler vanished three years ago. He

has never returned.

One cannot help but wonder if the Time Traveler will ever return. Was he swept back into the past to the Stone Age? Or is he viewing the reptiles of the Jurassic times? Or did he go forward to discover answers to the riddles of our own time? I know that my friend was eager to learn the secret of time. To me, the future is still a mystery, with some light shed, perhaps, by the Time

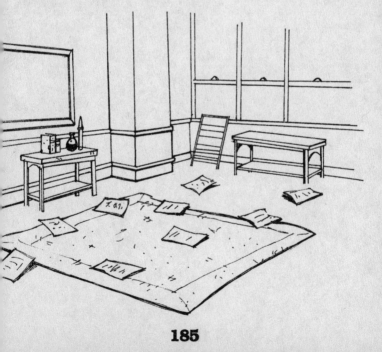

Traveler's strange tale and two dried-up white flowers. These stand as witnesses that even when human intelligence and strength had weakened, gratitude and companionship still lived on in the hearts of human beings.

# THE END

## About the Author

Herbert George Wells is considered by many to be the father of the modern science fiction story. He was born in Bromley, Kent, in England in 1866. Wells's father was a shopkeeper, and his mother, prior to her marriage, worked as a domestic servant.

In 1883, Wells began working as a teacher at the Midhurst Grammar School. Not long after, he enrolled in the Normal School of Science, in London. Later, Wells became active in politics. Twice he ran for Parliament.

*The Time Machine*, published in 1895, was Wells's first novel. The book's popular success, which continues to this day, allowed Wells to stop teaching and devote himself to writing. The three novels that followed, *The Island of Dr. Moreau* (1896), *The Invisible Man* (1897), and *The War of the Worlds* (1898) are also considered science fiction classics. Wells died in London in 1946.